KU-788-205

Kitsy Bitsy's Noisy Neighbours

Polly Faber • Melissa Crowton

What lovely homes in Park View Rise!
Those who live here truly prize
this modern block with great location,
handy for the shops and station . . .

but still so peaceful. Oh so quiet.

No-one here would cause a riot.

Honky Tonk and Hunky Dory
live up on the top-most storey.
Tonk's a singer, quite the diva.
Dory is a muscled beaver.

Together they're the
best of mates –
one trills scales and
one lifts weights.

"Tra-la-la!" and

"One, two, three!"

Dory jumps, Tonk hits top C.
Their thumps and high
notes travel down . . .

. . . to Tippy Toes –
they make her frown.
Her baby really needs a nap . . .

the noise has made his big ears flap.
And now he's bawling,

"BOO HOO HOO!"

He's heard below by
someone who . . .

. . . is working on his latest book.
Smart Alec finds his typing nook
is not a place to write with feeling
when there's wailing through the ceiling.

He gives up with a heavy sigh
and starts instead on DIY.
His power drill goes

JUDDER!
JUDDER!

making evvv-errr-yyy-thinggg shudder.

And swings a light
that's down one floor,

so . . .

. . . Rocky Locky cuts off more
than she meant to from Big Wayne,
leaving only half a mane.

As Rocky tries to fix the crop,
her scissors fly, they sculpt and chop.

Big Wayne wakes slowly
from his dream . . .

    looks in
    the mirror . . .

gives a **SCREEEEEEEEEEEEAAAM!**

His roar blows all
the scraps of hair . . .

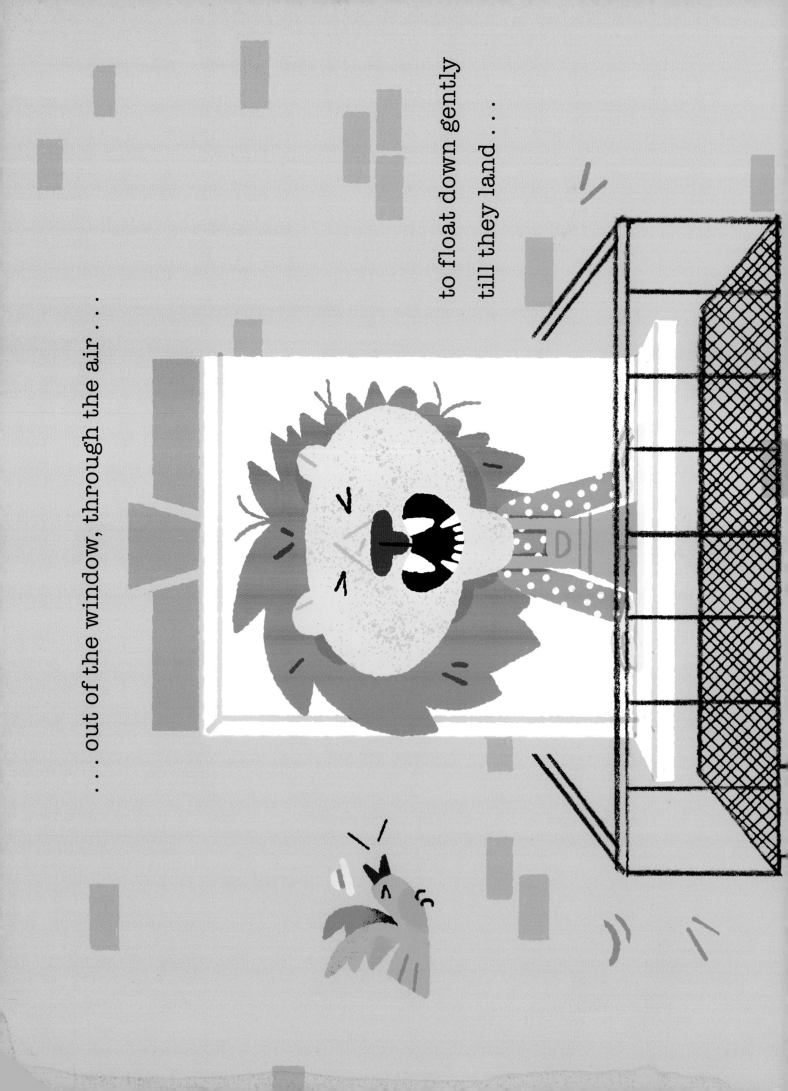

on Sugar Plum's
enormous stand
of fresh-baked buns
and sticky cake,

left there to cool – a **BIG** mistake!

Now tears stream
down his cheeks
and snout . . . .

. . . and Plum tips
all his pastries out!

Cookie crumbs
and icing goo
rain down on
Fiddle Faddle, who
is on her balcony
to mend a broken
scooter for a friend.

All the jammed-up parts get jammy.
So does Faddle – double whammy!

But on the ground floor of the block . . .

. . . lives someone, who, round the clock,
can sort out problems and disputes:

Kitsy Bitsy wears **BIG** boots.

And sensing trouble in the air,
she frowns and pushes back her chair . . .

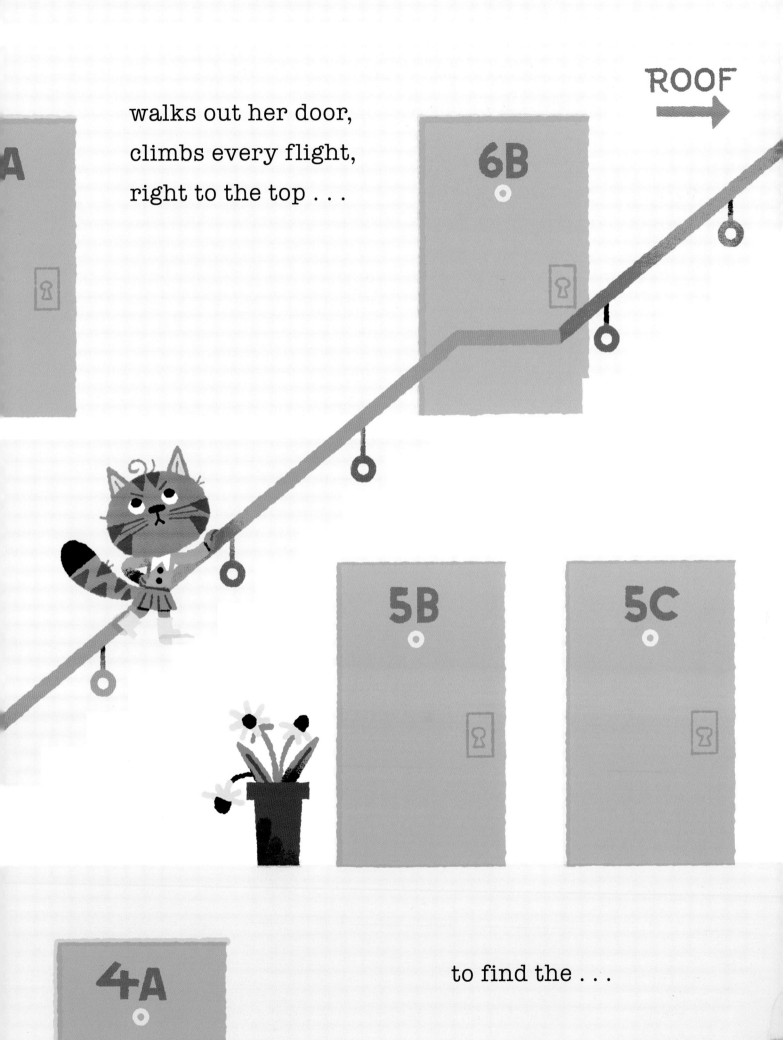

ROOF

A

walks out her door,
climbs every flight,
right to the top . . .

6B

5B

5C

4A

to find the . . .

. . . FIGHT!!

There's growling, yowling, yelling, crying!
Buttercream and sprinkles flying!

But Bitsy's made of steely stuff.
She lifts one eyebrow, says . . .

"ENOUGH!"

Straight away the neighbours halt.

They start to shout, "It's not **MY** fault!"

But Bitsy says, "I just don't care

how this began, you have to **SHARE.**

Be thoughtful, kind, or **ALL** of you

can find new housing at the zoo." So . . .

. . . Baby's rocked
by Hunky Dory.
Alec tells a
sleepy story.

Fiddle Faddle helps replaster
all the DIY disaster.

Sticky mess is
washed away
by Tippy's trunk
on power spray.

While Tonk
asks Wayne, with
his loud roar, to join
the band on their next tour.

And Rocky goes from home to home,
collecting . . .

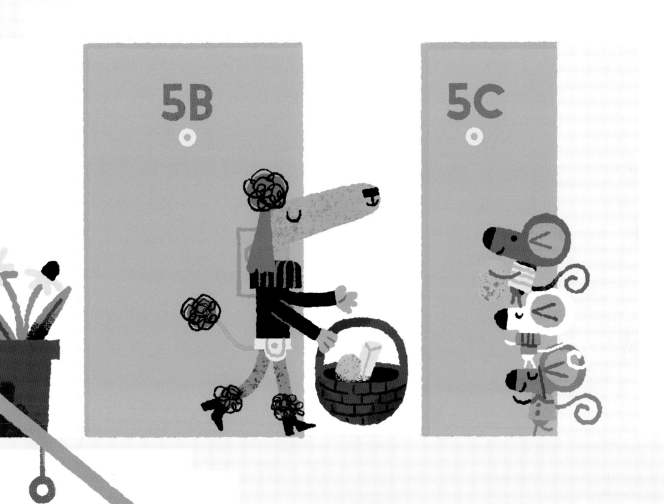

eggs . . .

milk . . .

honeycomb . . .

. . . Till Plum has all he needs to bake
a marvellous **good neighbours cake.**
And everybody has a slice,
agrees they'll be as quiet as mice.

But not just yet – it's **MUCH** more fun
to dance and sing with everyone!

And neighbours –

friends – forget, forgive . . .

. . . for there's **no place**
they'd rather live.

Good Neighbours Honey Cake

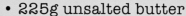

You will need:

- 20cm round, loose-bottomed cake tin
- Greaseproof paper
- Medium saucepan
- Wooden spoon
- Sieve
- Large bowl
- Wire rack
- Pastry brush (optional)
- Small saucepan

- 225g unsalted butter
- 100g muscovado sugar
- 250g clear honey, plus a bit more to glaze
- 3 large eggs, beaten
- 300g self-raising flour
- Icing sugar, strawberries and sprinkles (optional)

Method:

STEP 1 Preheat the oven to 160°C/140°C fan/Gas Mark 3.

STEP 2 Line the cake tin with greaseproof paper.

STEP 3 Melt the butter, honey and sugar slowly in the medium saucepan over a low heat until it's all liquid.

STEP 4 Increase the heat and boil for about a minute. Take off the heat. Leave to cool for 30 minutes.

STEP 5 Beat the eggs into the cooled mixture in the saucepan using a wooden spoon.

STEP 6 Use the sieve to sift the flour into the large bowl, then pour in the egg and honey mixture. Beat together until the batter is smooth.

STEP 7 Pour the mixture into the lined cake tin and put in the oven carefully.

STEP 8 Bake until the cake is well-risen, golden brown and springs back when pressed. Check after 50 minutes, but it may need an hour. Turn out on a wire rack to cool.

STEP 9 Warm a little more honey in the small saucepan and brush or pour over the top of the cake to give a sticky glaze. If you like, you can add icing sugar, strawberries and sprinkles.

STEP 10 Slice and share with your friends and neighbours!

> Always make sure a grown-up is with you to help with hot things in the kitchen.

For my neighbourhood Moai,
with love PF

To my nieces and nephews,
MC

First published 2022 by Nosy Crow Ltd
The Crow's Nest, 14 Baden Place
Crosby Row, London, SE1 1YW, UK

Nosy Crow Eireann Ltd
44 Orchard Grove, Kenmare,
Co Kerry, V93 FY22, Ireland

www.nosycrow.com

ISBN 978 1 83994 366 9 (HB)
ISBN 978 1 83994 367 6 (PB)

Nosy Crow and associated logos are trademarks
and/or registered trademarks of Nosy Crow Ltd

Text © Polly Faber 2022
Illustrations © Melissa Crowton 2022

The rights of Polly Faber to be identified as the author
and Melissa Crowton to be identified as the illustrator
of this work have been asserted.

All rights reserved

This book is sold subject to the condition that it shall not,
by way of trade or otherwise, be lent, hired out or otherwise
circulated in any form of binding or cover other than that
in which it is published. No part of this publication may be
reproduced, stored in a retrieval system, or transmitted
in any form or by any means (electronic, mechanical,
photocopying, recording or otherwise) without the prior
written permission of Nosy Crow Ltd.

A CIP catalogue record for this book is
available from the British Library.

Printed in China
Papers used by Nosy Crow are made
from wood grown in sustainable forests.

10 9 8 7 6 5 4 3 2 1 (HB)
10 9 8 7 6 5 4 3 2 1 (PB)

X090302

Kitsy Bitsy's Noisy Neighbours